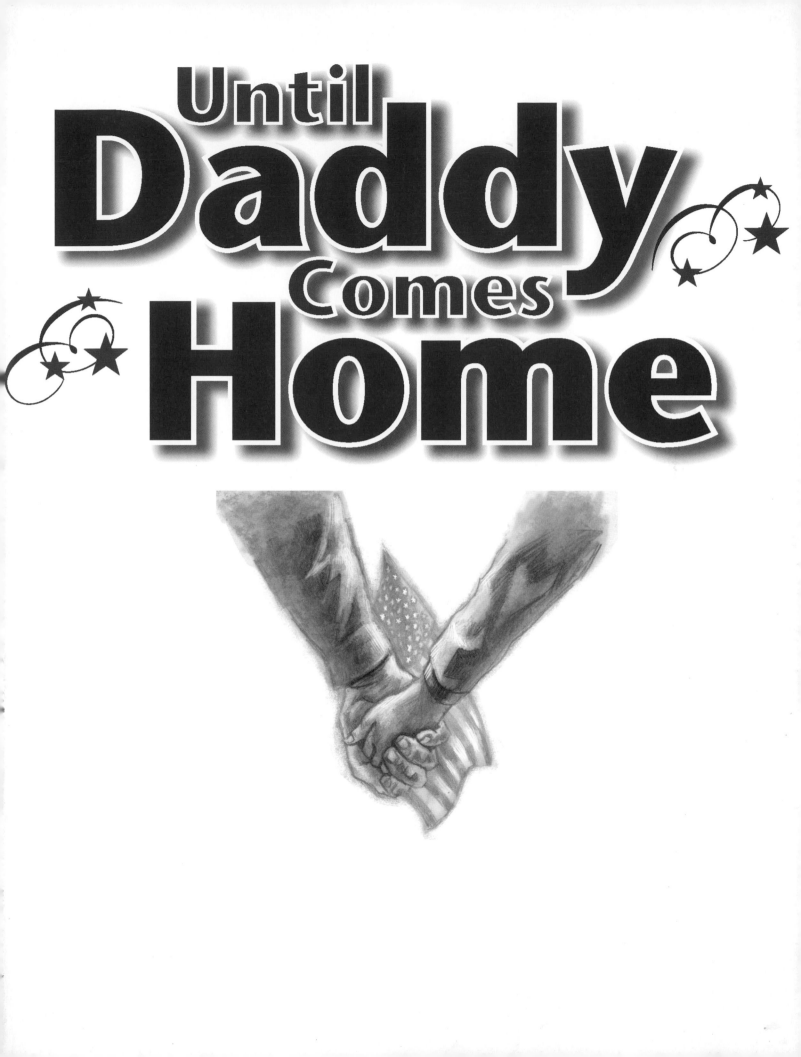

# Until Daddy Comes Home

By Gary Metivier

Illustrated by Robert Rath

PELICAN PUBLISHING COMPANY

GRETNA 2014

*To all of the families that have given up so much for all of us. Also to the USO and to other groups that work so hard to support our military families and our communities. To the countless volunteers who give of themselves to be there for those who need it most. Especially to Phyllis Root, Marsha Chall, and the Hamline family for helping with this salute!*

*The word "Pelican" and the depiction of a pelican are trademarks of Pelican Publishing Company, Inc., and are registered in the U.S. Patent and Trademark Office.*

Library of Congress Cataloging-in-Publication Data

Metivier, Gary.
  Until Daddy comes home / by Gary Metivier ; illustrated by Robert Rath.
       pages cm
  Summary: "A little girl watches as her daddy leaves to protect our country. But they have made a secret pledge to keep strong hearts. When Daddy comes home, they have a joyous reunion"— Provided by publisher.
  ISBN 978-1-4556-1890-3 (hardcover : alk. paper) — ISBN 978-1-4556-1891-0 (e-book) [1. Children of military personnel—Fiction. 2. Fathers and daughters—Fiction. 3. Patriotism—Fiction.] I. Rath, Robert, illustrator. II. Title.
  PZ7.M5667Un 2014
  [E]—dc23
                                                                        2013024517

*What is the USO? Established in 1941, the USO (United Service Organizations) is a 501(c)(3) non-profit, congressionally chartered, private organization that lifts the spirits of America's troops and their families by delivering highly valued programs, morale-boosting services, and engaging entertainment. With more than 160 locations, today's USO is always by the side of our troops and their families, continuously adapting to meet their needs around the world.*

Printed in Malaysia
Published by Pelican Publishing Company, Inc.
1000 Burmaster Street, Gretna, Louisiana 70053

Cameras flash in the school gym. The high school band plays. My eyes sting as my daddy walks away. He is going away to protect our country.

I can't cry. He said I could—but I want to stay strong for both of us.

Before he left, he told me, "Don't forget our secret pledge, Ashley."

We wrote **our pledge** together so that we can say it together—even when we are far apart. Every day after saying the Pledge of Allegiance, we both promise to close our eyes and whisper our secret words:

"I love you always, near or far.
We'll do our parts
and keep strong hearts.
I throw a kiss to where you are."

Then we'll throw a kiss to the flag. I can keep our pledge, but can it keep me strong while Daddy's gone?

"Quiz tomorrow on states and capitals," my teacher says. "Don't forget to study tonight."

**Homework** is harder without Daddy. I remember him drawing silly flashcards to make it fun. I still have the drawing of a giant baked bean marching in a parade in Boston. I'll never forget my capitals.

Maybe I can make my own silly flashcards! I'll even make some for the places where Daddy is right now, so he can laugh and learn, too.

One day down. So many more to go.

Candy-har

i ♥ I-ROCK

PERSian

BAG-DAD

This **morning,** I miss Daddy so much that my stomach aches. If I was sad, he would make me the "daddy special," a squeeze of chocolate syrup into my milk when Mom wasn't looking.

Today, I am going to make it for myself. When Mom turns away—*squirt*—I sneak some chocolate into my glass and take a big gulp. *Ahh.* I feel better already.

But only for a little while.

I'm trying so hard to keep our pledge, but it is hard work. Every morning, I whisper:
"I love you always, near or far.
We'll do our parts
and keep strong hearts.
I throw a kiss to where you are."

I can keep our pledge, but can it keep me strong while Daddy's gone? The hardest part of the year is coming.

I'm not very excited about decorating our **Christmas tree**.
Each year, Daddy and I pick out something new to put on
it. Usually, it isn't even a real ornament.

Last year, it was a pink plastic unicorn. We put it next to the purple hippo. Only Daddy and I know that the blue flying pig always goes at the very tippy top.

I bet he misses our tree. I grab my colored pencils. I draw our tree: a pink unicorn, a purple hippo, and a blue flying pig, at the very top, of course.

When Daddy gets it in the mail, it will make his heart stronger, too.

As the days go by, it is never the same without him here—especially for the...
**Daddy-Daughter Valentine Dance.**
This year, it is minus Daddy.

He's not here to pretend to faint when he sees me in a fancy dress; to bow and ask, "Care to dance, milady?"; to say, "That's okay. I have another one," when I step on his foot.

I dance in my room alone, wishing I could have just one dance with him. That would make me strong again.

"I can take you this year," Mom says, peeking through the bedroom doorway.

It won't be the same without Daddy, but Mom and I can practice his favorite dance, the Two-Step: *one step, slide, one step, slide.* Maybe when he comes home, I won't step on his foot so much.

I'm doing okay. I can keep our pledge, but
can it keep me strong while Daddy's gone?

Why do we have to talk about our parents on **Career Day?**

Mom comes to school with me to talk about being a nurse. Daddy is a zillion miles away.

"Before we begin," my teacher says, "let's stand for the Pledge of Allegiance."

There's a lump in my throat. My hand covering my heart is shaking. ". . . And liberty and justice for all."

It's time for *our* pledge. My eyes fill with missing-Daddy tears. But I made a promise. I made a pledge! I squeeze my eyes tight as I whisper our words.

"I love you always, near or far." I swallow hard. I have to keep going.

"We'll do our parts and keep strong hearts." I picture Daddy saying his pledge too. I can feel him! I can almost hear him!

"I throw a kiss to where you are."

I open my eyes and throw a kiss to the flag. "Caught it!"

I swing around.

"I'm home!" Daddy yells. My daddy! My very own daddy!

I jump into his arms and squeeze tight. "I remembered our pledge! It made my heart strong!"

Daddy whispers in my ear. "I'm so proud of you, Ashley."

"I'm proud of you too, Daddy. Our pledge made us both stronger."

"You've done such a great job without me here—but you still need me, right?" he asks.

I hug him again with my best bear hug, and Mom joins in.

"Daddy, I need you more than ever!"

Over his shoulder I see the flag. I blow it an extra kiss.

I kept our pledge, and it kept me strong...

**until Daddy came home.**

Not everyone is lucky enough to get a surprise like this at school. Many moms and dads return to a much more personal homecoming. Some families have to be apart longer than others. Those families sure could use some help staying strong for each other. That is where great organizations come in, especially the USO.

### A Note from a USO Director

Each of us has a home in our heart. No matter where we're from or what our life brings, home is that place that connects us to ourselves, a place that understands us, renews us, and welcomes us with open arms. For our military and their families, the USO is that place. In times of peace and in times of war, the USO has been a "home away from home" for our service men and women since the 1940s. The USO lifts the spirits of America's troops and their families and makes a true difference in the quality of their lives.

While many know of the USO through its beginnings during World War II with Bob Hope and lively USO Camp Shows and Canteens, the USO has continued to flourish through the decades, expanding its scope. Today, our mission remains the same and includes not just entertainment but also a full spectrum of programs and services that provide true resources and assistance wherever our military are serving around the world.

This global mission of the USO also is alive on the local level through USO locations across the United States that support the military and their families in their hometowns. The USO of Illinois provides hundreds of recreational and educational programs every year, a reliable link to resources, services, and respite from the daily stresses of military life. We deliver this support through direct outreach in the military community and at all of our USO center facilities, including USO Rock Island, located on our National Historic Landmark, Rock Island Arsenal. Opened in September 2011, USO Rock Island addresses the needs of the Quad Cities-area military community—serving thousands every year—and provides a vital bridge for the civilian community to get involved, volunteer, and show their patriotic support.

Whether local or global, home is where the heart is, as the saying goes. For our troops and their families, so bravely serving our nation on the home front and abroad, home is wherever the USO is.

Alison Ruble
President and CEO
USO of Illinois
*To learn more: www.usoofillinois.org*